LIZZY'S
DO'S
AND
DON'TS

By Jessica Harper · Illustrated by Lindsay Harper duPont

HarperCollinsPublishers

Lizzy's Do's and Don'ts
Text copyright © 2002 by Jessica Harper
Illustrations copyright © 2002 by Lindsay Harper duPont
Printed in the U.S.A. All rights reserved.
www.harperchildrens.com
Library of Congress Cataloging-in-Publication Data
Harper, Jessica.
Lizzy's do's and don'ts / by Jessica Harper;
illustrated by Lindsay Harper duPont.
p.   cm.
Summary: Lizzy and her mother take turns listing the kinds
of behavior they do and do not want from each other.
ISBN 0-06-623860-9 — ISBN 0-06-623861-7 (lib. bdg.)
[1. Behavior—Fiction.   2. Stories in rhyme.]
I. duPont, Lindsay Harper, ill.   II. Title.
PZ8.3.H219 Li   2002   [E]—dc21   2001024771   CIP   AC
Designed by Stephanie Bart-Horvath
1 2 3 4 5 6 7 8 9 10
❖
First Edition

For Elizabeth and Nora
❤ J.H.

For Sammy, Rosie, and George
❤ L.H.dP.

IT SEEMED
TO
LIZZY, ALL
HER MOTHER
EVER SAID
WAS
DON'T!

Don't shout indoors.
Don't tickle so hard.

Don't leave your party shoes
in the yard.

Don't take the deck
and lose one card.

Don't, don't, don't!

Don't climb in trees
containing bees.

Don't put 10 Band-Aids
on your knees.

Don't cut your hair.

Don't argue, please.

Don't try to reach what's out of reach.

Don't bring the sand home
from the beach.

Don't feed the kitty cat
a peach.

Don't, don't, don't!

Don't hold your breath

'til

you

turn

BLUE.

Don't lick the dog,
though he licks you.

Don't keep that lizard in my shoe!

"Okay, okay, okay, okay,"
said Lizzy. "It's MY turn!"

DON'T

say I can't do
so much stuff.

DON'T

huff and puff.

DON'T

say **2** chocolates are enough!

DON'T

act too tough.

Don't, **don't, don't!**

Don't make me wear that yellow dress.

Don't always say my hair's a mess.

Don't say no when you could say yes. Don't, don't, don't!

Don't hide my candy up so high.

Don't put nuts in the apple pie.

When I ask why, don't frown and sigh.

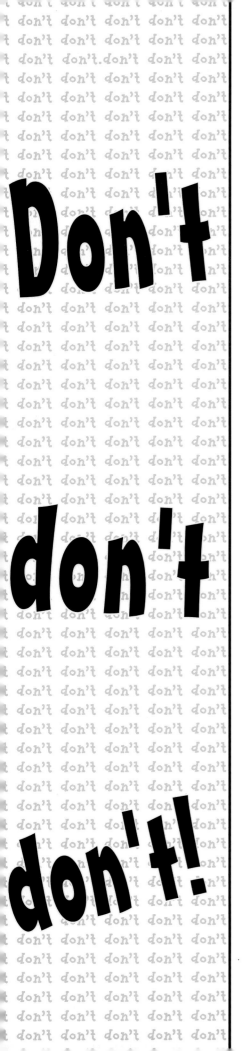

Don't
don't
don't!

Don't say to me,
"You should have known."

Don't **chat, chat, chat** on the telephone.

DON'T LICK SO MUCH OF MY ICE-CREAM CONE.

Don't, don't, don't!

"Okay, okay, okay, okay, okay, okay, okay!"
Said Lizzy's Mom,

"The word *don't*
is a tiresome thing to say!"

They thought about it
for a little while,
then Lizzy said . . .

DO

teach me how to be prepared.

DO hold me close

when I am scared.

DO

take my bike to get repaired. Do, do, do!

DO

help me dress up
like a wizard.

DO take me sledding
in a blizzard.

DO please let me keep
the lizard.

Do do do!

Do tell a fairy tale to me.
Do rock me gently on your knee.
Do, because . . .

I LOVE YOU!

Yes, I do, do, do!

Then Lizzy's mother smiled and said,
"Okay, now it's my turn."

Do climb a tree as high as you dare.

Do put some daisies
in your hair.

Do tell me when
life seems unfair.

DO, DO, DO!

DO please be

glad
or

mad
or

sad.

Do wear pink polka dots with plaid.

Do tell some secrets to your dad.

Do, do, do!

Do help me zipper up my dress.
Do tell me if my hair's a mess.
Do ask me if I love you. . . .